For A…

September
2016

with love

Pippa
Korens

The Pot with the Hole

Prem Rawat   Illustrations by **Aya Shiroi**

文屋
bun ya
Obuse Japan

Deep in the mountains lived a gardener.
His little house stood in the middle of the
garden he had planted and tended for
many years.

Every morning he walked down the path
to the stream where he filled two pots
with water for his garden.

With the pots full and balanced on either end
of a wooden pole, he carried them up the
path that led to his little house on the hillside.

Nearby animals often greeted them.

'Beautiful day!' a lark called out.

'Yes, it is the beginning of spring,' one of the
pots replied.

'It looks like heavy work,' a hedgehog called out.

'It is,' the other pot replied. 'And we don't want to spill a drop.'

The pots felt proud that they could help the gardener in his work.

But one morning, while carrying the water
up the mountain, the gardener slipped
and fell.

One of the pots hit a rock which made a
little hole in it.

'Oh no!' the pot exclaimed. 'I'm leaking!'

As the gardener continued walking up the path, the leaking pot, drip by drip, slowly emptied. By the time he reached the garden, there was very little water left in the pot to pour on the flowers.

Day after day, week after week, the same thing happened. Water leaked from the hole in the pot - drip, drip, drip - as the gardener carried it up the path.

Some weeks later as the gardener
was taking a rest, the pot without a
hole spoke to the leaky pot.

'You are completely useless,' he said.

The pot with the hole was upset.

'Why are you being so mean to me?'

'Because you're no good at all with
that hole in you.'

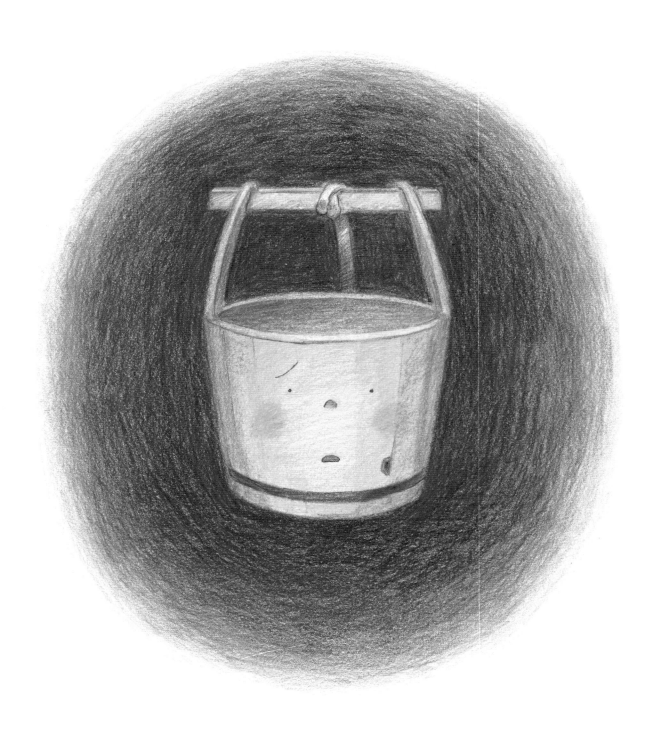

The pot with the hole felt ashamed of himself.
He felt he was no use to the gardener any more.

When the lark greeted him with
'Beautiful morning!', the pot didn't reply.

When the hedgehog started a conversation,
the pot said, 'I don't feel like talking.
Leave me alone!'

The hedgehog turned away as fast as his
little legs could carry him.

Whenever the gardener watered his plants, the pot with the hole thought:

'This garden looks so beautiful with its flowers and trees swaying in the wind. The gardener works hard caring for the plants, but so little of the water that I carry reaches the garden. He must be very disappointed with me.'

Finally, he could no longer hold back his tears.

The gardener noticed immediately and went over to ask what was wrong.

'Why are you so sad?' the gardener asked.

'Because of this hole in me! I can't do what I'm supposed to do. I'm useless.'

'It is true that you have a hole,' the gardener said. 'But that does not mean you are useless.'

'I am!' the pot sobbed. 'I can't even carry a full load of water to your garden.'

'Now, now,' the gardener comforted him. 'Listen to me. As soon as I realised you had a hole, I started planting seeds along the path. Thanks to you I can water those seeds a little everyday as we go back up the hill.'

The pot stopped sobbing.

'Take a look at the path,' the gardener said.

The pot with the hole raised his eyes
and was astonished by what he saw.

Along one side of the path,
magnificent flowers were in full bloom.

Bees buzzed around gathering nectar and
butterflies skipped from flower to flower.

The pot with the hole had been so caught up in trying to hide his leak, he hadn't noticed the change in the path.

For a while he just sat there amazed.

The other pot also saw how beautiful the path looked and he apologised for having been so mean.

The next morning, both pots were happy again.

'The path looks wonderful!' the lark called out.

'Good job!' the hedgehog said to the pot with the hole.

'I'm glad you like it,' the pot replied.

With a big smile, he went about his task of watering the flowers that lined the side of the path.

I was born and raised in northern India near the foothills of the Himalayas, where we have a rich cultural tradition of storytelling. When I was a child, not only my parents, but many different adults in our village would tell us stories.

My father was a well known speaker on the subject of inner peace and he would blend different stories into his discourses. My father passed away when I was eight and I took on his role of sharing this message of hope for humanity.

I remember I would be attending school like any other little boy during term time, but in the summer holidays I would tour India and address large gatherings of people around the country. People from other countries also began to take an interest in my message.

At the age of 13, I was invited to speak in London and Los Angeles, and I began travelling and speaking all over the world.

I have many stories that I share with people when I speak. Whatever the country and audience, people enjoy the magic of stories as a means of understanding something. *The Pot with the Hole* has such a beautiful message behind it that I decided it would be my first illustrated storybook.

As long as I can continue to travel and share my message with people, this is what I will be saying:

'The peace and happiness you are looking for is already within you. You only need to slow down and connect with it, to connect within yourself.'

August 2nd 2016
Prem Rawat

Prem Rawat

Prem was born in India in 1957 and from a young age has been speaking about a simple and practical peace that all people can experience within themselves. He left India at the age of 13 in order to share this message with people. Since then he has addressed live audiences of over 15 million people at events in 250 cities. His talks have been translated into 75 languages.

In December 2015 Prem released *Splitting the Arrow - Understanding the Business of Life* with Bunya Publishing and it continues to gain popularity, having already been translated into 15 languages.

2016 marks the 50th year since Prem started sharing his unique message of hope around the world.

More information about Prem Rawat and his message can be found at:
premrawat.com
timelesstoday.com

Aya Shiroi

A celebrated illustrator and animator, Aya was born in Tokyo in 1968 and graduated from Tokyo University of the Arts where she now teaches.

Her animation has been shown in a number of international animation festivals and in 1996 was awarded first prize at the BACA- JA Japanese animation festival.

Aya's work regularly appears on national television (NHK) in Japan. She has illustrated many best selling books and popular animated shorts.

With a versatile array of styles and mediums, her passion is touching people through art.

www.shiroi-aya.com

The Pot with the Hole

1st Edition release date September 19th 2016

Author	Prem Rawat
Illustrations	Aya Shiroi
Editors	Max Whittle
	Norman Silver
	Jo Robinson
Publishing	Bunya publishing corporation, LLC President Yutaka Kinoshita
	Prem Rawat's official representative for Japan
	45 Iida, Obuse-machi, Kamitakai-gun, Nagano Japan
	http://www.premrawat-japan.com/en
Design	Takeshi Shindo
Printing and binding	The Australian Book Connection
	27 Bowman Parade, East Oakleigh Vic 3166